this book belongs to:

_____

This title is also available as a Tate Out Loud product. Visit www.tatepublishing.com for more information.

Published by Tate Publishing & Enterprises, LLC
127 E. Trade Center Terrace | Mustang, Oklahoma 73064 USA
1.888.361.9473 | www.tatepublishing.com

Tate Publishing is committed to excellence in the publishing industry. The company reflects the philosophy established by the founders, based on Psalm 68:11,
"The Lord gave the word and great was the company of those who published it."

Published in the United States of America

ISBN: 978-1-61663-938-9
1. Juvenile Fiction / Religious / Christian / General
2. Juvenile Fiction / Religious / General
10.11.17

His Love for me is STRONG

story by Wivina John

Tate Publishing & Enterprises

Dedication

To my precious grandchildren, Kevin, Azeleah, and Celina, who are such inspirations to me. I trust God that they will come to know Jesus Christ as their personal Savior at a tender, young age.

Acknowledgment

To my daughter, for her adamant support, relentless encouragement, and belief in me, without which I would not see this material come to fruition. May God richly bless her.

Who was Jesus? Jesus was a baby just like I was. He had a mommy and a daddy like I have too. His mommy's name was Mary, and his daddy's name was Joseph. Jesus played just like I play, learned new things like I do, and was taught like I am taught. But there was something very different about Jesus. He was a very, very special boy who was born to do great things that people never did.

When he grew up to be a man like my daddy, he showed the people he cared for them. When people were sick, he made them well again. He also fed a lot of people with five loaves and two fish. He even walked on the water too.

But there were people who did not like Jesus. They made him carry a big cross a long way to a place on a hill. They beat him badly all the way. They put a crown on his head too, but his crown was not pretty like a king's crown. His crown was made with sharp thorns. Ow! That really hurt. But Jesus did not cry. The people placed Jesus on the cross and nailed his feet and his hands. They all laughed at Jesus while he was on the cross; but after a long time, Jesus died.

A man who loved Jesus took his body down from the cross and put it in a cave. The cave was called a grave. Jesus's body was there for three days; and after three days, he came alive again. You see, Jesus had told the people he loved that he would come alive again after three days; and he did.

The people saw him and touched him. Jesus stayed a little while with them, and then he went up to the sky. He is still alive, but he is in a beautiful place called heaven. He told the people he will come back again. They must tell everyone to believe he died, he was buried, and he is now alive again. When my daddy is not at home, I know I have a daddy even though I cannot see him. This is called believing.

God loved everyone so much that he sent Jesus to die for our sins. Jesus obeyed God because he loved me very much too. You see, sometimes I do bad things like taking what is not mine and not telling the truth. I am sometimes disobedient to my mommy and daddy.

Little people do small bad things, and big people do big bad things. Jesus calls all bad things sins and said they are wrong. Sins make him sad. Jesus said there is a place where people who do bad things go and live for a very long time. He said if I believe he died for my sins and tell him I am really sorry for them, I will not be punished. Someday, I will live in heaven with Jesus for a very long time.

Jesus gave us a big book called the Bible. It is just like a letter a daddy writes to his child when he is away. The Bible tells me that Jesus loves me very much and he will send a best friend to stay with me. That best friend is the Holy Spirit. Even though I cannot see him, just like I cannot see Jesus, he is with me all the time. He is not like my best friend who comes and leaves. When I go to bed at night, he stays with me so that I do not have to be afraid of the dark.

Jesus wants me to talk to him just like I talk to my friends. He wants me to tell him when I do bad things too. He wants to forgive me and help me not to do them again. I can talk to him when I am sad and when I am happy too. Talking to Jesus is called praying. Jesus loves me very much and is never too busy to listen to me. He wants to listen to me all the time. I can be God's child if I tell Jesus I am sorry for all the bad things I have done.

I can pray and ask Jesus to come into my heart and forgive my sins, if I am really sorry. I will pray like this:

"Dear Jesus, please forgive me for the bad things I have done. I believe that you died to take the punishment for all my sins. You are alive again and want me to live in heaven with you some day. Please come and live in my heart today. Jesus, I love you very much. Amen."

God loved the world so much that he gave his only son, so that anyone who believes in him will not die but will live forever.

For God so loved the world that he gave his only begotten son, that whosoever believeth in him should not perish but have everlasting life.

John 3:16 KJV

THE

END

e|LIVE

---

listen|imagine|view|experience

AUDIO BOOK DOWNLOAD INCLUDED WITH THIS BOOK!

In your hands you hold a complete digital entertainment package. In addition to the p
per version, you receive a free download of the audio version of this book. Simply u
the code listed below when visiting our website. Once downloaded to your comput
you can listen to the book through your computer's speakers, burn it to an audio CD
save the file to your portable music device (such as Apple's popular iPod) and listen
the go!

How to get your free audio book digital download:

1. Visit www.tatepublishing.com and click on the e|LIVE logo on the home page.
2. Enter the following coupon code:
   06b8-7ccd-8765-77b5-412b-788a-ad1b-14b2
3. Download the audio book from your e|LIVE digital locker and begin enjoying your new digital entertainment package today!